Ricca, Brandt. *Barris and the Prince of Rappa.*

Copyright © 2021 by Brandt Ricca

Illustrations by Matt Miller

Cover layout and book design by Liona Design Co., www.lionadesignco.com

Published by KWE Publishing: www.kwepub.com

ISBN (hardback): 978-1-950306-89-3
ISBN (ebook): 978-1-950306-90-9

Library of Congress Control Number: 2021914956

THE BARRIS BOOKS

BARRIS
and the
Prince of Rappa

WRITTEN BY
Brandt Ricca

ILLUSTRATED BY
Matt Miller

Table of Contents

"To the path that led me here, and all the stories I heard along the way."

— BRANDT RICCA

"To my mom, for always helping to bring the creative light out in me."

— MATT MILLER

1

Chapitre Un...

Once upon a night...somewhere behind two little eyes and between two little ears, and at the top of a tall green house, was the dream universe of Barris Hart...

In that universe that he entered each night while he slept, were different worlds that intersected for a moment. Characters resided there of all sorts...but all were magical, nonetheless.

My name is Gracie. I am Barris' guide through those worlds and your guide through this book...but we will fruit loop back to me later.

It was 1952 New Orleans where nine-year-old Barris lived with his family, the Harts. They moved from Washington D.C. the previous year. Barris, his mom and dad, and three sisters relocated because Barris' mother, Francine Hart, discovered her ancestry was French. And upon this discovery, she became obsessed with everything that was related to France.

. . . .

New Orleans in the 1950s was the perfect place for someone who doesn't know much French but wants to be surrounded by the culture. French was heavily spoken there, and the city wreaks with "tout Francais!" (everything French). So, the Harts packed their bags and moved to support their mother on her quest to feel close to her family ties. New Orleans was different all on its own and was most certainly different from Washington D.C.

Mrs. Hart took French lessons, French cooking classes, and even referred to their very tall green house as the "Eiffel Tower." It stuck out in a row of close-knit houses and was the tallest, with a giant staircase that went right up the middle. Barris' room was at the very top, as he was the only boy and could have his own space. The Harts resided on Frenchmen Street. Sounds of jazz musicians inhabited the atmosphere more than the people did. It was like having a soundtrack to your life when you took a stroll.

While Mrs. Hart prepared dinner on a late September afternoon, she fed the dog, Oliver, a fat, short-legged Jack Russell terrier...whom she called, "Olivier." She frequently inserted her newfound culture (in her case her newly learned French accent) into everything she came across.

"Olivieeerrrr, it's time to eat," she would say daily.

At the same moment that Francine Hart was making dinner, Barris hopped off the trolley from school and ran with his backpack and his "pack," as he called it, around his waist down Chartres Street and turned onto the street where he lived. His brown curly hair tossed beneath his favorite red hat when he looked left and right, with his little blue eyes, to avoid traffic while he vroomed into his neighborhood. "I love it here," Barris thought when he passed all the brightly colored architecture on the street.

A week earlier new neighbors had moved in across the street. A very tall family, the Longthistles. They looked different from Barris and his family, with their olive skin. They were of a different descent. What, you may ask? Barris couldn't figure it out, one he never encountered before. But he heard tunes blaring often that weren't French or English, and smelled delicious food from their open kitchen window.

Glenda, their daughter, had a neck as tall as a leg and arms to match. She was in the same grade as Barris, but he was the size of an ant compared to her. Her purple overalls and black pigtails were the only things that seemed soft about her appearance. She and her family were of ginormous stature and matched their last name.

Longthistle...

Barris was a bit scared of her due to her size, and every time she approached him to try and play in the neighborhood, he would run away screaming, "Gotta jet! Au revoir!" (that means "goodbye" in French). He would make his two friends Dean and Pevy run away from her with him, though they never understood why. Glenda would always appear disappointed and would turn to walk back to the swing set alone on the school playground, her head hung low.

• •

Dean and Pevy were Barris' first friends in New Orleans. Dean was a skinny, shiny-complexioned looking boy with stringy brown hair. Always in a long sleeve button up. Dean liked to deem himself proper. Pevy had long brown curly hair and crystal blue eyes, always dressed in what looked like boy's clothes. She was very athletic. They were normal by any definition of the word, usually innocent bystanders of Barris' irrational actions, but supportive, nonetheless. And they supported Barris through his paranoia with Glenda.

What Barris noticed that afternoon when he turned onto his street, was that Glenda was not out in her front yard like usual. When he realized this, he hightailed it into his "Eiffel Tower" house. *"PHEWWW,"* his mind processed when he slammed the front door behind him, which caused Oliver to bark with excitement at the sound of the door. When he leaned on the door that closed behind him, he felt his quickly beating heart slow down.

THUMP, THUMP, THUMP...THUMP...Thump...thump.

"Mon fils!" Mrs. Hart exclaimed, (French for "my son"). Barris executed his daily eye roll at his mother, and he went upstairs to wash his hands for dinner.

Inside the Hart residence it was warm. Warm with light and atmosphere. Mrs. Hart had bright gold drapes on almost every window that were very fluffy and touched the floors. Old red oriental rugs were in almost every room, but the kitchen, and all of the furniture was "comfy and cozy" Mrs. Hart would say. When they moved into their new home, Mrs. Hart had put purple wallpaper inside the house everywhere, a lavender shade. On the wallpaper were beautiful white designs that resembled tree branches of different sizes.

"Did you have a good day?" Mrs. Hart asked when she approached the staircase and caught the back of Barris' head. Mrs. Hart was a bigger than average woman and had curly short red hair. She could always be found with an apron around her waist and wore her mother's pearls with everything she did. Out to parties...or to clean the toilet.

"It was just a day," he said when he passed his three sisters in their respective bedrooms. Betsy, Betty, and Bernice were their names. Betsy and Betty were older twins with curly blonde hair and freckles. They did everything together and shared a room. They had princess canopy beds on each end, and everything was pink...and they were "too much" in Barris and Bernice's opinion.

Bernice was more like Barris, she was a year younger, similar in all ways but her appearance. And the fact that she was a loner, one could say her only friend was Barris. They understood each other without having to exchange words. Bernice had black hair, was short for an eight year old, and was pale in skin. She was often found in a corner of the room reading.

"Hey BERNice," Barris said when he walked past her room. He knew it annoyed her to say her name like that and he didn't want to miss the chance to annoy her on that day.

At dinner an hour later that night, the Hart family dined on their mother's latest French cuisine, *Coq au vin*, a recipe she no doubt learned the day before in her cooking class. Mr. Hart spoke of his day and all that entailed with his business.

Their dinner table was a long dark wooden table. It was shiny and took up almost the entire dining room. As they sat between their purple wallpapered walls, the Harts always dined around candle light. On the walls were other lights coming out of them, "Why are there fake candles on the walls?" Barris asked on move-in day. Mrs. Hart would look at the "fake candles" (that were just lights on the wall), and the real ones she lit every night at 6:00 p.m. when she set the table and commented almost each time "Oh doesn't this all just feel so romantic?" No one ever answered, it was like she was always asking herself.

"Today was a busy day, dear. I had meetings all over town, with all kinds of people." Barris' father, Conrad Hart, ran his own company. Barris didn't really know what the company did, nor did his sisters. All they knew was that he made a lot of money and carried a briefcase. Mr. Hart was a skinny, tan man (from always doing yard work on the weekends, he loved to be outside gardening) and was always in a white button up and a sweater vest. His mustache was long and black and curled at each end like a pirate's would. Sometimes at dinner when Barris stared long enough at his father's face, he would picture him on a pirate ship, kidnapping people, sailing the seas, or looking for buried treasure as he twirled the end of his mustache with his fingers.

"Shiver me timbers!" Barris would picture his father saying as he spoke to people at work.

"That's great, cheri," Mrs. Hart would say whenever she would acknowledge what Mr. Hart was saying. "Cheri" means "dear" or "honey" in French.

"Has anyone seen the new girl across the street today?" Barris asked the table. "She normally is always outside in her front yard, but I didn't see her."

"Barris and Glenda sitting in a tree…K-I-S-S-I-N-."

"Nuh uh!" Barris interrupted Betsy and Betty before they could finish spelling the word, as they sang together.

"Mother, tell them to stop it."

"Now leave Barris alone," Mrs. Hart said softly to the girls. "Barris you need to ask little Glenda over to play. It's hard being the new kid in town."

"There's nothing little about her," he replied. "She's so tall I heard that at her last school the teachers made her skip a grade because they were scared of her."

"That's utter hogwash," Bernice said. She finally looked up and engaged, while her head was in a book at the dinner table. This phased no one.

"I remember a little boy who was once new to town also and wanted someone to play with before he had any friends." Mr. Hart looked across the table at Barris and gave him a lowering eye. They had moved just six weeks prior to New Orleans. Barris was put into a group for a school project with Dean and Pevy, and made friends with them easily that way.

Barris looked down at his plate to finish his last bite of his meal. "I suppose," he said, and he reluctantly agreed with his father.

After dinner, the family all chipped in with the dishes as the sounds of Edith Piaf played in the background. No one knew a word of her music, but hummed along anyway to show support for their mother. She's a famous French singer so naturally Mrs. Hart was obsessed with her.

The dishes were of all bright colors, red, blue, and yellow, which seemed to go along with their yellow and white tiled kitchen floor. "Colors make life more fun!" Mrs. Hart would tell the children anytime they were all out and shopped together. Bernice was not a fan of her mother's saying, as she always wore dark colors. "You like black because it's the color of your soul," Barris would tease her.

After dinner, Barris brushed his teeth and crawled into bed. Barris closed his eyes and thought about what his mother and father said. Maybe he should try to get to know Glenda.

"You can't always judge a book by its cover." Barris flashed back to Bernice telling him that just a few minutes earlier, as she walked past the bathroom door. Barris hated that saying.

He then heard his parents talking downstairs, while his dog Oliver laid at the foot of his bed. Barris liked when Oliver slept there because he kept his tootsies warm. Tootsies were what his mother called feet. Barris' room was blue, with pictures and maps of all the places he would like to visit someday. His father joked often that his room was a life-sized globe.

Barris then dozed off to sleep. Right before he heard his mother laughing as the music played, while she tried to sing along (out of tune) to the words she didn't know, and danced with Mr. Hart in the living room below.

• •

2

Chapitre Deux...

Now everyone enters their dream universe differently. From the moment the first child was born and fell asleep it has been so. Your surroundings influence your entrance into your world while you slumber. I know of a little girl in the Amazon who hitches rides on raindrops that carry her over waterfalls to her dream universe. And of a little boy in London who dings amidst his room in the air, until he flickers and POOFS away with the tick-tocking of Big Ben at midnight.

For Barris...the sounds of jazz in his neighborhood on Frenchmen street vibrated through his bedroom walls, and carried him away on the musical notes of "la la la, la la." That's tres New Orleans, ("tres" is French for "very.").

On the wave of the musical notes, Barris passed all of his favorite things: Oliver, his short fat Jack Russell terrier; his favorite red hat that he grabbed to put on his head along the way; and golden leaves that swirled around him... Autumn was his favorite time of year.

Tonight, Barris got carried away to Rappa...

After a whimsical ride, Barris opened his eyes and felt that he had landed on something soft and fluffy. "It's a marshmallow!" Or so he thought as his hands sank down into the softness when he pushed himself up. In the dream world, they had plants and flowers of all sorts. Some were rooted to the ground, while others floated in different colors depending on their origin. Barris had landed on a Synnfor (SIN-FOR). They were light blue, pretty, and floated like clouds, so to Barris' credit, they did resemble marshmallows.

"Where am I?" Barris thought.

He always had dreams that he remembered; they were always pleasant and fun. Full of things that children dreamed about. Things that they forgot about when they were older. But this night was different. Barris had just turned nine. The age where innocence can start to become lost and childish enthusiasm starts to dwindle.

Barris stood up to find his bearings and he dusted off his blue and white striped matching pajamas, his red hat and his brown fuzzy slippers. Around his waist was an old leather "pack." It was his grandfathers when he was a Boy Scout and he had given it to Barris the year prior.

His grandfather had made it himself as a child. He needed something useful and convenient when he ran around the woods and earned his badges to hold his things. It had everything you could think of in it for emergencies. Barris wore it everywhere, even to sleep! He had experienced an earthquake in California visiting his grandfather. It happened in the middle of the night, so to help Barris feel "ready for anything" his grandfather gifted it to Barris. Barris would call it his "pack." Bernice always made fun of him for it.

Barris walked around and realized he was in a garden. He needed to find an opening, which he did, so he started to step one foot slowly in front of the other on the narrow, cobblestone paths that zigged and zagged in front of him.

Colors of red and green leaves blinded his eyes as he looked up at the blue and gray sky. When he focused further, he saw a distinct difference where the blue ended... and where a gray began. It was like the sky was split in half.

He walked through the garden path and past the exotic plants and pushed open a gate door to discover the world outside the black iron bars. The gates made a loud screeching noise, which caused Barris to cover his ears. The gate appeared to not have been opened in FOREVER.

"Rappa," Barris read on a sign that was carved on an old pole outside the garden. The worn, faded wood spoke to its age. Barris then said it out loud, "Rappa."

The garden faded behind him when Barris walked to the front of a castle, a castle that had seen better days. It was as if a shadow was upon it. Barris was hesitant in this strange new world to do any exploring, but his curiosity was persistent. As was with most people.

I heard once that you should always "wake up curious and find where curiosity takes you."

Next to the dark castle and the colorful garden in the background where he woke up was a gray area, which was the rest of the world of Rappa. He walked to the gray-colored streets which were on the side of the castle and saw that there was no one in sight. The bakery had no baker. The candle shop had no candlestick maker. "Gee whizz, where am I, and where is everyone?" he thought.

Something had happened here in this quiet place. It was obvious. With no visible person in sight or anything lit up, Barris had to enter the castle that he first stood in front of moments earlier. Admittedly he wanted to go in there anyways.

· ·

Barris pushed through the castle doors, which was a struggle because they were so big and heavy, the air brushed up from underneath them. In doing so a huge sweeping sound of whispers filled the front of the castle.

"psss, pssss, pssss, psssssssss."

Barris had awakened the dust mites who had been asleep for some time. Now they were all abuzz to know who was there.

On hearing the dust-mites, I, Gracie, ran downstairs because I was already in the castle doing an inspection. I'm from Norizon. In Norizon we can see all the other worlds in dream universes of all sleeping children and we can see when something isn't right. Think of Norizon like the dream headquarters. We monitor all the dreams of each living child until they reach the age of ten. When a child turns ten, they start maturing from childhood.

I had seen that the world of Rappa had gone from bright red to gray, which was never a good sign. It meant the world had lost its purpose. **Rappa had lost its purpose for six weeks now.**

I am a Keeper of the Universe. I come from a long line of great Keepers, where our jobs are to monitor all dream universes of every sleeping child and to make sure everything is always running smoothly, dreamily. My grandmother Lucy was a legend. Everyone in all the different dream universes knew of her. She is long gone now and just a memory. I want to be just like her, which is why everywhere I go I wear her great big brown coat. It's a bit dusty, but it helps me get the job done nonetheless because it holds all my investigative supplies. It doesn't match my blue- and white-striped knee-high socks or my slip-on dark green shoes, but my fashion statement doesn't have to make sense. Moreover my head is full of red hair that looks like spaghetti I've been told, and I wear a black beret to try and keep the curls in place. All of this sits on top of my purple eyes. My eye color and black skin allow people to distinguish me from others in the dream universe. My appearance tells others that I'm important.

I heard the dust mites when Barris entered and it alarmed me. Dust mites were so chatty and gossiped about everyone they saw and heard everything. They were EVERYWHERE! I sprung high from step to step to check on the noise.

Keepers got to have all sorts of abilities (some more than others depending on your level of cases solved, they're almost like rewards to help you serve dreams better), and I was able to travel with big leaps and it helped me get around easier...and it was fun. I was new to this work because I just reached the Keeper starter age of nine.

I got higher with each leap and I saw Barris' blue eyes widen as I looked down at him, and then he blinked at least five times and he shook his head in disbelief.

When I reached him, I said, "Hola! I'm Gracie!"

3

Chapitre Trois...

H ola?" Barris asked me. He appeared puzzled.

"It means 'hello' in Spanish. I know children all over the world, Barris Hart, and I've picked up a thing or two. Like 'bonjour' means 'hello' in French."

Barris already knew what "bonjour" meant from his mother, and he rolled his eyes.

"Oui, oui," he responded back, which showed me he understood some French.

We stood in the middle of the castle. The floor beneath us was full of swirls, but not many together. They were peach colored that appeared to be faded, and they spun in clusters of five. The LARGE foyer of the castle was full of clusters of those swirls on the floor. It made me dizzy to look at them for too long.

I had leaped down from a tall staircase that went up the side of the castle. The stair swirled up all the way to the top.

. . . .

So high that you couldn't see where it ended. Throughout various parts of the staircase were hallways that would lead to other areas of the castle. But boy, aside from the loud little dust mites, the front of the castle felt so quiet and empty. Our voices echoed as words left both of our unsure lips.

"How do you know my name? Who are you?" he asked me.

"I am a Keeper of the Universe, and it is my job to make sure all of the worlds in the dream universes of children are running smoothly. Right now, it's your universe, Barris, that's off course. I hail from Norizon and I came down the instant I knew something was wrong, and lo and behold, the Prince of Rappa is missing. I need to find him and restore Rappa to its glory. I also knew you were here from the dust mites...loud little things. I'm here on a mission."

"What kind of work? What happened here?" he asked when he looked around amid the dust mite chatter. "Where's the prince?"

"So far, the only information I have received is from the dust mites. They have told me that he had a fight with the Princess of Menos."

Menos (MIN-OSE) was the neighboring world of Rappa and the prince and princess were best friends. Menos was also a world in Barris' dream universe. But, there was a disconnect between the two somehow.

"For the wickety of me, I can't see why they would argue. Whatever has happened, two things are for sure: The prince is missing and the Emmes (IMM-ESSE) River,

• •

connecting the two worlds, has stopped flowing. No one can get in. Or out."

"How come I've never seen you before in my dreams?" asked Barris.

Typically, his dreams were full of sweet things. One fun encounter after another. A sweet box, within a charmed box, was usually the pattern of dreams of young children before the age of ten, unless it was a unique situation.

"There has never been a need for me to appear and help solve issues in your particular dream universe, Barris," I told him, "I've seen and been in other children's, but not yours...but I'm new, as well."

Each Keeper was assigned different children and Barris was my first case alone. Growing up on Norizon, I worked in the shadow of my grandmother, Lucy, who lived her life as she restored each dream world, inside each dream universe of lots of children. She was no longer here: I was next in line in my family to take over.

Each child had his or her own keeper when needed, and Barris had never needed one prior to tonight. He had just turned nine a couple months earlier, after all! He was close to the threshold of ten.

I told Barris all of this and the dust mites got into a tizzy of whispers again and we saw a large shadow from the castle hall approach from upstairs. When the shadow approached and got closer, I realized it was the Queen of Rappa.

Her large, red transparent royal robe draped down her back and spread out to the side as if she had butterfly wings. The robe was a part of her being. It was attached to her like an arm or a leg, it hung off of her light blue skin.

She got closer to Barris and me, and I saw her eyebrows raise, they showed concern and her crown sat on top of her orange flowing hair.

"Gracie, darling! I'm so glad you're here!"

Everyone in the worlds of Barris' universe knew who I was, and that I was following in my grandmother Lucy's footsteps.

Flashback

Two feet walked behind a curtain, with black heeled shoes, green and white striped socks, and a familiar big brown coat. As the curtain opened, a woman with a glow all over her shouted, "Queeeeeen!"

The woman had black curly hair, all pinned up on top of her head like a bird's nest. She had rosy black cheeks and thick black eyebrows, and piercing purple eyes sat beneath them.

"Oh, Lucy, thank you so much for all you have done for the King and me," the Queen of Rappa told Lucy, who was sitting down in the royal suite where she was with the queen. Drapes of plush purple and gold were all around them.

"But of course, queen, it is my duty to make sure everyone is always happy in their respective dream worlds."

• •

They both sat in lavish style as they sipped tea, pinkies in the air, of course.

"I'm sweeping through all of my worlds before I go to spend some time with my granddaughter, Gracie. She is three and always begging to come along with me on my journeys. You would think she was three going on 'knowing it all,'" Lucy said.

"From the sounds of it, she is just like her grandmother."

Fast forward to Barris and Gracie

"Your Highness."

I bowed and pulled at Barris' white and light blue striped pajama shirt to bow with me.

"Gracie, the prince has disappeared, vanished. But not before he stopped the flow of the Emmes River and my husband, the king, cannot get back home because of it. A dust mite told me that they saw my son speaking with Grelda right before he vanished from sight, and the flow of the Emmes River along with him."

Grelda was the witch of THE dream universe, meaning she was involved in every dream universe, of EVERY child. Everyone knew who she was. She wasn't known for always making the best decisions or casting amazing spells. Either way, that was a clue that would help me further solve my case.

"Your Highness, I will sort this out and get your son and your husband home. I have assistance with me. This is Barris, a Keeper-in-training."

I fibbed because I knew the queen wouldn't allow a complete stranger to be in her castle meddling in Rappa business. Barris looked at me confused when I spun him around, which caused his pack to slide down to his knees. I pushed him past the queen and through the sound of the loud dust mites, and we jumped over the threshold of the castle.

"Off we go. I will report back soon," I shouted to the queen, as I tried to believe the words that came out of my own mouth.

"Hurry, Gracie! It is vital that you bring back my son!" the queen shouted when her words echoed through what sounded empty castle halls, when the doors closed behind us.

4

Chapitre Quatre...

We stepped outside the castle near the garden where Barris had woken up, looking at the gray covered Rappa next to it. I explained to Barris why I didn't tell the truth to the queen. I told him that moving forward, he was to go along with my story and do anything else I told him to do, he was a "Keeper-in-training."

"The queen doesn't know who you are," I told Barris. "She is very protective of this world and wouldn't like a stranger being up so close to the window of the royal family. She learned that lesson once before."

*Flashback*

The queen and Lucy were sitting in the royal suite enjoying their tea, when a loud noise that sounded like an airplane flying over occurred, with a big flash of light barging

. . . .

through underneath the royal suite's door. The tea spilled out of the cup Grandma Lucy was holding.

"What was that?!" the queen shouted.

Earlier that day the queen had an unknown stranger show up who she had not known. Now strangers being in Rappa was not unusual, but to have a stranger get to the castle doors and to have an audience with the queen was very unusual.

The stranger was found wandering around the castle grounds and was there to sell the royals his latest invention. He looked very odd. Eyes that went cross-eyed, brown pants, and a green jacket with a long red tie that was tucked into his belt. He wanted to sell a new bridge to the royal family that would be laced with magic and would only allow those with good intentions to cross.

The queen was curious about this man and his sales pitch, so she allowed him to work on setting up the bridge for a demonstration, while she met with Lucy.

The man seemed nervous and swallowed a big "GULP!" when the queen agreed. It was as if he didn't expect her to.

Fast forward to Gracie and Barris

"So, you see Barris, the queen now is just weird when it comes to strangers being around."

"What happened? Did the bridge work?" Barris asked me.

"Nope, it blew up when he tried to seal it with magic, and the queen is far too busy to deal with such nonsense.

• •

So that was the last straw of her entertaining unknowns in her castle."

He agreed to go along with my fib and so I then immediately started my investigation. I had to trace the prince's last steps before he disappeared.

"We have to solve this case, and we don't have time for all the questions about who you are and why you're here."

Throughout Rappa, it was mostly gray except for the garden where Barris had dropped into when he fell asleep that night. Magic always kept the garden's beauty as it was the center of this particular world. There was a glimmer of light from the craftsman's shop. Surely Keppy, the town carpenter, saw something.

We ran there instantly.

"Gracie! And the answer is?" Keppy asked, he assumed I solved the mystery of Rappa already, and he whisked his fingers down his knee-length blonde beard.

He spoke and while he did, he was constantly stroking his beard like he was in deep thought. His hairy face made his bald, shiny head stick out more. You could almost see your reflection in it. He was always in a messy white apron that was stained with dirt from him sawing wood.

"Working on it, Keppy. This is Barris, a trainee who I am showing all the things of a Keeper's job. When was the last time you saw the prince?"

"It's been ages, actually. I was so busy with people coming from the other worlds, I haven't had a chance to keep up with the royal family. But I did hear he had a spat with the Princess of Menos and that he's behind the mystery of this mess."

"How do you know all of that?" I paused. "Never mind." I knew it was the dust mites.

"You know who you should take your curiosity to? Leda," he said, and he stroked his beard.

Leda was the teller of fortune in Rappa who tended to know all.

"Good thinking!" I shouted and I leapt away from Keppy, and urgently headed towards Leda.

I had to be swift with this mystery.

My reputation was on the line!

Leda's tent was on the other side of Rappa and we had to get there quickly.

I ran and I jumped and kept forgetting that Barris didn't have my leaping ability, so I kept grabbing his hand and pulled him up into the air with me. With each jump that passed, I would look at Barris to make sure he was still hanging on. His eyes looked beneath him in awe.

I saw Barris amazed by my abilities and it made me realize I should be amazed, too.

"Pretty neat, huh?" I asked him.

"Be thankful and aware of what you have, and you will already possess everything," my grandmother Lucy would always say.

• •

We take things for granted that we are accustomed to and don't appreciate them. Sometimes we forget them.

Up in the air, we saw all of Rappa and the tops of the trees. They were all grayish green, but as we whisked by them we caused the leaves to twirl all around us like wind tunnels.

I spotted Leda's tent. It wasn't hard to miss. It was big and purple, and in the shape of a triangle. I knew she would be able to help us.

How did I not think of her first?!

We landed in front of her tent, and we started to walk down a path of sparkling green emeralds that led to the entrance.

When we approached it, we pulled back the cloth of her tent slowly, to see if she was there.

"Shush, don't make any loud noises. I don't want to spook her before we talk to her."

"You're so bossy," Barris told me.

"You'd be bossy, too, if you had a case to solve and your Keeper career depended on it," I whispered back to him.

I removed the purple draping, and it exposed the inside of the tent which was full of light and warmth. She was the teller of fortune, after all. Of course, her surroundings would be that of magnificence. The gray that covered Rappa could not affect her.

We walked in and I could see Leda—well, the back of Leda at least. Her black hair was long, as long as could be, resting in a pile of swirls. It was French braided and had large red rubies in them that were spiraling down. We could see our faces in them with each bright sparkle. She wore a long flowing amber glittery skirt that touched the floor, with a ragged white shirt tucked in, green eyes sat below her black hair.

She was steadily working on something, but we could not see what it was. In the corner were her busy Tikas (TEE-KAS) who were working on a variety of tasks she had clearly delegated to them.

Tikas were short, hairy dirty blonde creatures that were a gift to Leda from the King and Queen of Rappa for all her good work. They were third cousins of the royal family that lived to help others. They were of good nature and assisted Leda with all her work.

Leda loved them all as if they were her children. She had them dressed in the most luxurious of things, colorful large smocks, jewels on their wrists. They never uttered a word, however. They preferred their actions to speak for themselves.

The fireplace that faced her, illuminated all the riches of shiny objects she had around her. The objects looked like things that filled Egyptian pyramids.

"Leda...Leda...Leda!"

I had called three times before she heard me. When she turned around, her long hair whipped from behind her and created a breeze that shook everything inside, blowing the purple draping in whooshes. All you could hear were the clacks of gold objects hitting each other. Barris' pack flew off his waist as my spaghetti red hair struggled to stay in my beret.

"Gracie, dear one, I was expecting you."

This came as no surprise to me, as Leda knew everything. There were rumors that circulated in the dream world that she had recently met with Grelda, the witch with whom the Prince of Rappa had reportedly just had an encounter. That is why Leda had more than the normal amount of beautiful objects in her possession.

Grelda clearly had been making her rounds with the people of Rappa, that was one thing for certain. No one knew why she had been talking to Grelda. Leda's tent almost had no room to stand from the objects.

One fact was that Leda had always been an admirer of beautiful things.

After I introduced Leda to "Barris, my trainee," I told her, "We are looking for the prince. We need him to tell us what he and Grelda spoke about and if it had anything to do with what is happening. No one can get in or out of Rappa, including the king."

"Yes, yes, I know all about that, though I haven't left my tent. No reason to, I have everything I could ever want in here."

With a fire in her eyes from the bright vibration of the shiny goods around her, her voice turned from soft and sweet to deep and creepy. Then chirped up again to soft and sweet.

"I do not know the whereabouts of the prince, but last I saw him he was over by the library of Rappa, wearing a hood and looking as though he were up to no good."

"The library? I guess that's next on our list to go and do some snooping around."

All of that was a start. I took all of it down in my notebook that I had kept in my big brown coat, and Barris had wandered away from me. I saw that he was touching something of Leda's, something very nice, a crystal on a huge chandelier.

I immediately ran over to grab him because I knew she would not like him touching her treasures.

"Barris!" I sternly whispered. "Leda is very possessive of her things, come back here!"

But before I could stop him, Leda shouted, "GET AWAY FROM THAT!" and whipped her hair around so hard that the wind from her large French braid picked Barris and me both off the ground and blew us out of the tent and outside, where we rolled down the path of green emeralds.

5

Chapitre Cinq...

She was acting more cuckoo than usual," I told Barris and we stood up to dust ourselves off.

I stared at Barris and my gaze went behind him to where he looked blurry and out of focus. I saw the Myoo (MY-YOO) of Rappa in the distance.

The Myoo of Rappa, which was what Leda called the library, housed everything of historical significance that had ever happened within the world of Rappa.

My instinct was to leap there immediately. I picked Barris up by my hand and scooped him up in the air with me again.

"Let's go! This way!" I shouted and Barris was startled by my grabbing him so abruptly.

We went above all the trees again and we could see the little beings that lived down inside the treetops. By that

• •

time, it was nightfall, so the trees were lit up with light, while the Mimas (MEE-MAS) sat down to dinner.

Mimas were droopy-skinned little creatures who lived in trees and gardens and took care of them, nurtured and loved them. They had quite the green thumb and anything they lived in blossomed. My grandma Lucy loved having them in her rose garden.

We landed down in front of the Myoo and ran up what felt like 100 white stone steps. The Myoo was a rectangle-shaped, white stone building. Large circular pillars decorated the building all around it.

I felt my legs were getting tired with each climb of a new step. "Can't you just leap us up?" Barris asked me.

"I could, but just because you can do something doesn't mean you should, Barris Hart. It's okay to put in some of the work."

The Myoo was so GINORMOUS that it looked as if it could house giants. Finally, we reached the door. I went to open it and when I did, it swung open slowly, and creaked with every inch.

I expected to hear the dust mites but remembered that the Myoo was sacred, and therefore, dust did not live there. It was kept up quite nicely. When we walked in, we were greeted by floating books that opened to specific pages, with the events on those particular pages playing out on top of them. It was almost like a movie scene that replayed on top in golden light.

Those books documented all-important things that had happened in Rappa... There was the time the king defeated the flying dragon and saved Rappa from its breath of fire. There was the time the queen negotiated peace between the troll mermaids that lived in the waters between Rappa and Menos in the Emmes River, which resulted in the Princess of Menos and the Prince of Rappa becoming best friends. The troll mermaids now helped the royal families with travel.

Green light illuminated the entire library and shiny particles sparkled in the air, like floating diamonds that twinkled. You could just feel the history in the building. This was where stories and legends were told, where they were stored and kept alive after they had long been over. "If only people could be kept here," I thought when I looked around and remembered Grandma Lucy.

Barris was being nosey, which I learned was a trait of his. I saw him when he walked and read the sides of the closed books that were on the shelves. All the pages were lined with gold and silver. You could almost cut your finger on the sharp edges. "DON'T TOUCH ANYTHING," I assertively told him.

I could see no sign that anyone was there. Everything looked in its place.

Barris walked backwards, mouth open, one hand on his waist holding his pack, and looked at the books that also lined the ceilings. He was in such wonder that he had stopped in stillness. "This is all so brilliant," he said. "Bernice would absolutely lose it here if she saw this. She LOVES books," he said when he looked over to me and then looked back up to the ceiling.

All you heard in the moment was that Barris exhaled. He then took one step back with his right foot and, unbeknownst to him, stepped on a gold plate-like thing on the floor, which caused him to disappear from my sight.

I ran up to find him and I felt his arm pull me into the invisible area, "Gracie, in here!"

We were in what seemed like a small book room of sorts; it was very dark with candles lining the sides of the wall. I had never seen anything like that before or heard of it from anyone in my family who had been a Keeper. An invisible space in the library of Rappa with secret rooms. "What is this place?" I asked Barris, like I expected a knowing answer.

"I don't think we are in Rappa anymore," Barris told me.

All at once, there was a huge commotion, caused by our presence that had disturbed the space Barris stumbled upon. Books separated and created pillars with pages that came out of other books and formed walls and a path.

I could see no end down the path that had been laid out in front of us made of papers, just black down the end. We started to walk. I was sure we would find the prince down the way. I could feel it. Grandma Lucy would say, "Follow your gut...look for the signs. When one doesn't pay attention, one strays down the wrong path."

BARRIS AND THE PRINCE OF RAPPA

"Be careful," I told Barris when we walked down the path. They were pages of books after all and not stones we were walking on. "We could easily fall through."

"I'm always careful," he said, "Rappa just sneaks up on me."

We started to walk down, and all seemed fine. We walked with ease and got about halfway...then the pages started to tear if we were on them for more than a second. I grabbed Barris and made a run for it. While I ran Barris couldn't keep up and flew through the air as I pulled him like a wet noodle behind me. I ran as fast as I could on my tippy toes trying not to fall through the pages.

"Don't let go!" I shouted back to him.

Through our flight, Barris reached down into his pack, grabbed a strap out of it, and threw it around his and my locked hands to hold us together. "I won't!"

I ran so fast I didn't see that the path ended in front of us, and we immediately fell and tumbled with pages circling all around us. As we fell Barris' grip loosened on my hand, and our fingers held on to the others with all our might. When this happened, we were still connected by the strap Barris had attached and we were both just tethering next to each other. "I'm also always prepared, Gracie," he told me as we fell further and further.

"Now is not the time!" I shouted and held my beret on top of my head.

We fell into some unknown wooded area, at least unknown to me. It was a dark place with fields of tall skinny trees. You couldn't even see the tops of them. A purple and greenish light covered the background and sky above us. We had landed into a small clearing.

Upon our fall in the ominous place, the pages of the books started to attack us. They hit us with every move we made when we tried to stand and open our eyes to take in everything. "OWWWW!" I shouted as a page cut me.

I saw Barris reach into his pack and he put on a pair of old sunglasses to cover his eyes. "UGH!!" he shouted proudly as he secured them on his head. He looked at me as if to say "seeee," referencing his preparedness.

The pages swarmed around us. I saw a large tree in the distance that had a little opening at the bottom of it. It was the thickest tree in the forest and stood out. My instincts told me we had to get in there to get away from the wrath of the books. I didn't want any more paper cuts...they hurt! I ran with the same speed as before and pulled Barris with me. "Let's go in here!"

We arrived at the opening of the tree. "You're crazy! I'm not going inside of a tree!" Barris shouted at me sternly.

"It's this or stay out here and who knows what will happen!" I grabbed the side of the opening of the tree and I immediately slipped inside and pulled Barris with me... we then fell down...again.

We landed in a silent, cold space. I fell on my face and swallowed a little bit of dirt. Barris fell on top of me, which didn't feel good. We had fallen about ten feet into what was almost like some sort of rabbit hole. "Are you OK?" I asked when I was met with, "That was so weird! What was

· ·

all of that?" Barris asked when he put his sunglasses back inside his pack.

My eyes adjusted to another new environment. I saw nothing but darkness, except for a small light, which was a lantern and a hammock that lay in front. That was it.

In the hammock I saw black hair and light blue skin peeping over.

6

Chapitre Six... (but with a French accent)

It's the prince!" I shouted to Barris when we stood and brushed dirt off and collected ourselves from our tumble.

From my loud antics of excitement, the prince was startled.

The prince's name, I forgot to mention, is Thomas. Prince Thomas of Rappa.

"Who's there? Who is it?" He flipped out of his hammock and fell on the floor, where he hit his head hard. He stood up and his vision was blurry before it came into focus. He stood there, he looked at me, "Gracie?" His eyes widened.

"How did you find me? Why are you here? Who's that with you?"

. . . .

I told him everything that had happened in Rappa, that the Emmes River that connected Rappa and Menos was gone. "Your father is stuck, and no one is able to get in or out. This is Barris, he is a Keeper in training."

More importantly, I told him that I heard he and Grelda had been talking and I thought he caused everything.

He looked as though he were about to yell at me, but instead let out a deep sigh and hung his head. His black wavy hair fell and covered his face. The prince had light blue skin like his parents, and wavy black hair that swept his forehead back and forth. He was short in stature and wore a yellow shirt, with brown pants.

• •

For the next while we all sat around a lantern and he told us everything...

"The Princess of Menos, Princess Nora, my best friend," he looked at Barris to explain who she was. "She changed her appearance. The Princess was coming into her time to rule her world, and for her parents to retire." He kept talking, but not making eye contact as he played with the dirt that we sat on and moved his finger in zig zags and drew random lines.

I interrupted him to explain to Barris that, "in this universe whenever a prince or a princess is ready to take over from their parents and rule their dream worlds, their appearance changes."

Prince Thomas then interrupted me, "The Princess, who had been short with freckles and with black short hair and light blue skin, transformed into a woman with huge wings as her robe, like my mom's, the Queen of Rappa. Her hair is long now and wrapped up in her crown, and with her new appearance she carries herself with a poise that wasn't there before."

"With a 'je ne sais quoi,'" I said and looked at Barris. That means with a "I don't know" how to describe it.

The prince was not ready to rule Rappa; therefore, his appearance was still the same. One morning when the two met for their usual frolicking among the garden in Rappa (where Barris awoke), the princess' new appearance frightened Thomas. For he no longer saw her as she used to be, plain Princess Nora. She was bigger than he was.

• •

"I ran away from Nora almost immediately when I realized what had happened. I realized that she had crossed over to the next stage that all children must cross, and I hadn't. In my anger, I summoned the universe witch Grelda to Rappa."

*Flashback to Prince Thomas
in the garden of Rappa*

Prince Thomas is running through the garden with his hands up as if he were an airplane and his arms were wings. As he is running, he leans his body from side to side "flying" among all the marshmallow blue and light pink bushes.

The prince sees an orange and yellow glow coming from outside the garden gate, but he thinks it is the sunset. As the glow gets bigger and closer, he sees a being enter the garden. Her long black hair draped down to her shoulders and then back up again sitting inside a crown. Big transparent wing-like things are attached to her back radiating the glow he sees. The robe is blue and purple and mixed together as if two paint cans have been dumped onto it. When the prince looks at her face and sees the princess' notable black mole next to her lip, he realizes it is Princess Nora and what has happened.

The prince's face turns red, and with his wide eyes he then snaps his finger (royals have all sorts of leisure abilities to get what they want on demand), he disappears from the garden in front of Grelda...the witch.

• •

Fast forward to the prince who was talking to Barris and me

Prince Thomas told us, "I frantically made a request to see Grelda due to Nora's transition, and I asked to run away and not have Nora be able to get to Rappa. Out of fear, out of shame. I was intimidated by Nora's new appearance and was ashamed that I was not yet at the point of being ready to rule myself." He wanted to get out of Rappa and he became swept up into seclusion, with his parents not able to see that Nora had been ready to rule and not him. He didn't want them to be disappointed in him.

Insecurity holds the puppet strings to many people; as a result, irrational behavior occurs.

We sat there and we kept hearing waves of the wind outside hitting against the tree from which we fell in. The sound of the branches that snapped were insane. It hurt our ears and Barris kept covering his. You could hear rips of the pages still swimming around in the air.

"We have to get out of this tree and find Grelda to make all as it should be in the world of Rappa," I told the prince, and he agreed. He also wanted to make things right with Nora and make sure his father could get home.

Finding Grelda would be easy, but for the one thing which we were about to find out.

7

Chapitre Sept...

W e didn't know where Grelda the witch was, so we had to figure out a way to track her through the rift in the dream universe that had been created upon her agreement with the prince.

All I knew was that Grelda would appear whenever you really needed her, so I asked Prince Thomas to try and summon her. He closed his eyes and he squinted hard and held his fists down at his side. Nothing happened.

"I don't understand," he said. "Last time, she appeared the instant I thought of her."

Being a Keeper, I knew from all my training that I had a bit more pull in the dream universe than the prince did. I had never summoned Grelda before, or anyone for that matter. But that moment was as good a time as any.

"Let me try. We don't have much time."

Barris stood there and gave me a look that said, "What do you think YOU are going to do?"

I closed my eyes and put both of my hands over my heart. I remembered what Grandma Lucy used to say: "Always lead with intention and the answer will appear."

I thought about all the things in Rappa that needed to be fixed and that I wanted to help. I opened my mouth and a slow whisper escaped it.

"Grelllllllda."

Barris and the prince looked all around in a panic waiting for her to appear.

Grelda was a witch of all sorts. She was known throughout all the dream universes of every child and was constantly sought after. She was short and had black and blonde hair and yellow skin. The top half of her hair was black, and the tips of her hair were blonde. She wore a long dark purple dress while on witch duty that covered her feet and it almost made it seem like she was floating and not walking. You never saw her feet. Witches are bound to nature. It's where they get their magic. The stories told were that their feet were roots, like at the end of trees or a plant. Though no one I knew had ever actually seen witches' feet to rule out this myth or not.

Her outfits were constantly changing and evolving according to her mood. If she was in a happy mood, her dress would turn as yellow and bright as the sun on peak day. If she was sad, then her dress would evolve into blue, a blue as dark as the saddest tear.

I tried saying her name again.

"Grelllda." I whispered.

When I did, a spark happened, and I saw a blink of Grelda. It was almost like a window opened and then closed quickly.

I grabbed the prince's hand to see if we could get a longer glimpse if we both tried. "Let's try all together." I knew Barris wanted to see the witch also, so I grabbed his hand too as the energy of his intention to help would be an asset.

The three of us stood there and stared into the open air and in unison we said, "Grelllda."

The window opened again and swallowed us inside and shut behind us.

I opened my eyes and I looked down and saw that my hand was still holding Barris'. I looked at my other hand and Prince Thomas was no longer there. I looked onward and I saw him running towards Grelda, who was in a big field of the brightest flowers I had ever seen, of all sorts of colors. All of the landscape looked like plush bedding you could sleep on but made of flowers. The sky was one big beautiful paint-brushed sunset.

Grelda had a basket in one hand and was picking flowers with the other. She was wearing a long red dress, the most elegant, sparkly thing. Her hair was in loose curls tied back. Something of her essence seemed different from what I had known of her before.

I looked at the vision that she was, and something came over me where I felt so relaxed. I closed my eyes slowly and then opened them up again the same and looked around in awe and felt nothing but tranquility.

"What is this place?" Barris asked me.

"I don't know, and I know all of the places there are, first the room in the Myoo, and now this!"

Barris yawned and started to stretch; a lazy grin took over his face.

I had to kind of shake myself out of the relaxing moment to focus on the task at hand, which was to have Grelda fix Rappa.

I grabbed Barris' hand tightly and I leapt towards the prince and witch.

"Grelda! Grelda!" I heard Thomas shouting as I caught up to him just when he encountered her.

"Thank goodness!" I joined in.

"How did you get here and more importantly, WHY are you here?" Grelda asked us, shocked and almost looked a bit disappointed to see us.

I saw her look at Barris, and I knew she knew who he was, for how could she not? She knows all as the dream universe witch. And this was Barris' dream universe, after all. She didn't say anything, though, or acknowledge his presence, really.

After we embraced her, she told us why she was in this flowered place.

"When I created the division of Rappa and Menos by stopping the Emmes River for the prince, something happened that jolted me to this place, a sort of limbo that was created by me doing a spell of such magnitude."

She had the power to leave but realized that it was difficult for people to summon her due to her being in that limbo, and she rose to the opportunity to take a break and relax in the newly created nirvana.

"It has been the most pleasurable experience, the happiest of ones," she relayed to us.

I told her all that happened and that we needed to get back and fix everything. She then realized her responsibility in all of it and that she needed to leave this temporary and heavenly home of hers. She dropped the basket of flowers and with that her hair started swirling.

Sparkles flew up from behind her, her curls floated in the air, and then they dropped down to her straight blonde and black hair color.

Her red, muffin-like dress then went from long and poofy to long and narrow, and turned from red to dark purple. She meant business.

Grelda then pulled out her finger and started to give it a whisk.

"Everyone hang onto each other now and stay close. Who knows what might happen, the way things have been going around here."

Her finger went slow and twirled and sped up like a tornado and created a wind tunnel with sparks flying everywhere. I literally blinked for one second and I saw that we were in the castle of Rappa.

When I blinked after I saw the castle of Rappa...the dust mites' chatter started entering all our ears.

8

Chapitre Huit...

We were back in the castle, and I saw the queen rush to us. Her long wings of a robe flew behind her like a kite on a windy day. She knew from the loud ruckus of the dust mite chatter that something or someone was back in the castle.

The queen brushed past the dust mites, and she was so fast her robe looked like she was flying when she swept the dust mites up into a whirlwind and made their sounds louder as they flew around in the air.

She hugged Prince Thomas, and she was so abrupt grabbing him that her robe swung forward, twirling around them and covering them both like a blanket.

"Thomas! My son—what did you do? Where did you go?"

"Your Highness, we don't have time for such catch-ups, we must see to it that your husband can get home and that Rappa and Menos are connected once again by the

Emmes River," I told her, "with all due respect, of course—
Queen Ma'am, Ma'am Queen." I was nervous when I spoke
so sternly to her.

Grelda went outside, stood on the castle steps, and
raised her finger. Before she gave it a flick, she looked back
at Thomas and asked, "Prince Thomas, do you hereby wish
to undo what you wished to be true?"

Prince Thomas nodded, and hung his head, still ashamed
by what he had done. His black hair, with his long front swoop
covered his face as it did when we first met him.

Grelda swooshed her finger in almost a figure-eight-
like motion, and sparks started to appear all throughout
Rappa. You could see the bridge that used to be, and it
started to be recreated again, and connected Menos and
Rappa. The water started to flow, and a brush of air whisked
through the entire world. The wind blew off my black beret
and Barris' pack, he needed to secure that thing more.

Within minutes, the King of Rappa came around the
castle, pulled in his water buggy by the troll mermaids, who
were not the friendliest of creatures. They were as loyal
to the king, though, just as much as they were rude.

The king was a big broad man, with a medium sized
crown with salt and pepper hair nestled into it. A cape hung
off his back that glowed like a flashlight off of his light blue
skin. All royals had blue skin to show they're distinguished.
Kings had capes that protected them and showed others
who they were. It also gave them the ability to shield others

or those around them in case there was danger. It was so long, it was tucked into the buggy like socks in a drawer.

"My son." The king looked down to Thomas. "I knew from the royal council what had happened. You mustn't make rash decisions like that ever again, especially when it affects so many. Royals, and others, cannot conduct themselves in such a manner."

• •

When the king spoke those words, we knew that because the prince had behaved the way he had, it further proved that he was not ready to rule the world of Rappa, and still had much to learn, which was ok.

"I promise."

I patted Prince Thomas on the back, and I walked over to Barris, who looked confused.

"What about the prince and princess?"

No sooner than the words left his mouth did Princess Nora appear in her new grand glory. She carried a sparkling stick, like a cane, and was dressed in her new crown and long robe like Thomas' mother's, the Queen of Rappa.

She walked over to Thomas and had to kneel to talk to him to be at his height. She had sprouted taller, becoming the Queen of Menos.

"I am I, and you are you. Everything we are, we are but true."

That was their motto they would say to each other in moments of self-doubt.

Thomas stepped closer to look into her eyes. I could tell he wanted to search for a semblance of his old friend. He looked deeper into her gaze and he stood still for a moment. A white sparkle went off in her stare that illuminated the front of his face.

"There you are."

9

Chapitre Neuf...

I walked out with Barris through the front of the castle. Behind us were the newly mended and connected royal family of Rappa and the Princess of Menos with her old friend.

"What about Leda?" Barris asked me.

"What about her?"

"You told me she is the teller of fortune, but she was acting very odd, wasn't she?"

When Barris said this, I recalled the rumors I heard about Leda making a deal with Grelda.

After it was brought to my attention, I whistled Grelda over to us before she spelled herself wherever it was that witches lived.

The wind once whispered to me as it blew through my red spaghetti hair that witches lived in the Dasa (DAH-SA) dream world. The Dasa dream world was filled with trees, plants, and woods of all sorts. It was a mixture of a rainforest and a jungle, which made sense because witches drew their power from nature. Also, the wind, like the dust mites, chatters and tells you all sorts of things. Grandma Lucy used to call the wind "the whispers."

It's a funny thing, your surroundings. Whether it is the wind or a dust mite, everything is always speaking to you.

After I told Grelda everything that had happened with Leda and her odd behavior, Grelda confirmed that she had a meeting with Leda where a deal was made.

"I could sense that Leda was going off track with being a teller of fortune. She was only telling people what they wanted to hear in exchange for goods as payment. I presented her with the opportunity to have everything she wanted, and in return, she had to uphold the duties of her job. She had to tell people all of the good truths they wanted to know and always have good intentions, and not take payments from them."

When Barris and I heard this, we could tell that Leda was not keeping her end of the bargain. She appeared to have all the things Grelda had spoken of, but she also had more from the people seeking knowledge from her.

"Greed blinds one's mind so often. Upon coming back into this world of Rappa from limbo, my intuition flooded back over me. I knew that Leda had not been honest with you about what had really happened with the prince when she knew. I've already made her gold and lavish items disappear. She will have a hard time ahead of her, but a needed lesson nonetheless."

. . . .

I thanked Grelda for her work and all that she did, and made her promise not to ever stay in a limbo again; it would make my job a lot easier if she didn't.

"You know how to keep a new Keeper on her toes," I told Grelda when we bid her adieu.

Barris and I started to walk to the garden of Rappa from which he entered as Grelda disappeared within a blink of our eyes. It was almost morning time in Barris' world, which meant he was going to be waking up soon and leaving Rappa.

"I don't want to be like the prince," he told me.

I looked at him, confused.

"There is a new girl, Glenda, who moved next door, and she scares me because she is so much bigger than me. I haven't been the nicest to her."

I let my face drop into a kind of gentle, relaxed expression that gave Barris the impression that it was ok...and that he knew what he needed to do when he looked at me.

"Barris, we all have things and people in our lives that seem scary or intimidating when we don't have all the information. It is the unknown that scares us. Is she nice? Will she like you? Will that brown banana taste bad?"

"What?" Barris looked disgusted.

"Hey, I was in a rush to get down to Rappa to meet you and that's all I saw in front of me for a pre-Keeper-duty snack."

"You're right, I haven't really spoken to her to know who she is, she always seems to want to play. My best friends

Dean and Pevy think I am crazy because they always want to talk to her," he relayed, and sounded ashamed.

"It's ok, you know what to do. We all let fear make us do strange things, as you have seen here. If you do what's right after you realize it, the other stuff doesn't matter from before."

Barris and I nodded to each other with the mutual understanding of what he was going to do. When we nodded, everything around Barris, me included, started to slowly fade with rainbow-colored sparkles everywhere.

Like sprinkles being poured into a cloud.

10

Fin...

When Barris woke up, Oliver was licking his face. He stretched his legs and arms to escape from under the covers of his bed.

"I hope the prince will be alright," he thought as he wiped his eyes of the "crusty stuff," as he called it.

The smell of bacon consumed his nose, which meant his mother was in the kitchen.

"La la la, LALA, laaaaaa."

He heard his mother performing her usual off-tune vocals.

Barris sat up and yawned and looked outside his window from his bed.

Through this window he saw Glenda's purple house across the street. He thought back about the Prince of Rappa and the Princess of Menos, and Barris knew he shouldn't have judged Glenda...or acted cruelly towards her.

Basing your opinion of a person based on their appearance automatically determines one's character and personal truth. That is not energy you want to put out into the world or your surroundings.

Thoughts are things, they get into the wallpaper in your room, into your favorite jacket and hat, and they take over your life. You must be careful and pick them out each morning like you do your clothes.

Barris now understood this when he stared at the house across from his tall green one...and he wrinkled his brow with determination. He sprung out of bed on a mission.

He threw on the blue and white striped t-shirt that was lying on the chair at his desk, his brown shorts and pack, along with his favorite red hat. He ran down the stairs with a purpose while Oliver chased him and barked with excitement.

Mrs. Hart chuckled very loudly with a French accent thrown at the end of each sound. "Oh, Olivier, calm down, s'il vous plaît." That means "please."

Barris ate his bacon next to Bernice, who watched in sheer disgust at how he gobbled it down with his toast. She peered up from the book she was reading long enough to judge. When Barris finished his breakfast, he left the table in a rush but held his glass of milk and chugged it as he walked. He placed it down by the front door and the cup left a milk mustache. Mrs. Hart wiped it away while she forced him to give her a hug and kiss.

"Mother, I have to gooooo!" he said when he tried to break free from her hard hold of a hug.

"Have a good day, beloved," Mrs. Hart said to Barris when she walked past Bernice and patted her head. Mr. Hart had already left for work early that morning.

When Barris swung open the front screen door, he pushed through it, leapt off the porch, ran down the tall staircase in front and jumped over the last three front porch steps. He ran past Betsy and Betty who were drawing on the sidewalk in chalk.

"Quelle surprise," (what a surprise) he thought when he saw they were drawing in pink.

He ran past them and towards Glenda's front door. When he approached, he stopped his fast-paced run to a slow walk up to the house. He already felt a layer of sweat take over his body from his jolt over.

He waited for a moment, before he pushed in the doorbell.

"Just do it, don't let this fear control you," he thought to himself remembering the prince.

Ding dong ding. The vocals of Pedro Infante, a popular ranchera singer, who sang songs which were the traditional music of Mexico, filled Barris' ears from the Longthistle house, along with their doorbell chime.

When each second passed, Barris heard his heart beating out of his chest and felt the sweat taking over his body more.

Heavy footsteps approached and they started shaking the front porch, Barris started to possibly regret the olive branch endeavor. The door pushed open so hard that his favorite red hat blew off onto the ground. He winced and closed his eyes from the sudden movement.

When he opened his eyes from the wind that just brushed past him, all he saw were big legs in front of him. His gaze followed the legs up to see that it was Glenda's father who was almost as big as their house. Barris couldn't make out his face because the man was SO tall.

"Hi sir—I'm your neighbor and I go to school with Glenda. Is she home by chance?"

What Barris heard next didn't sound like words, but a loud mumble. After about ten seconds of the mumbling he heard in the background, "Coming, Dad!"

Glenda then appeared in front of her father's legs.

"Bonjour, Glenda! I mean, *HI.*"

Barris was embarrassed that his mother's French was attaching itself to him.

"So, I know that you're new to the neighborhood, and to New Orleans, and I think we have homeroom together at school. I was wondering if you wanted to walk to school with me and I could show you the ropes of Hynes Elementary. That is, only if you would like."

Her eyes widened with shock and excitement.

"Thank you...that would be great!"

It looked as though her eyes glossed over with tears that built up. She grabbed her backpack and shouted up to her father that she was going to school.

A loud mumble answered her back.

Barris always took the trolley home from school, but in the mornings would walk because it wasn't THAT far, and his mother didn't mind him walking with friends in the light of day a few blocks in the morning. But he had to take a trolley home.

When they walked off the steps together, Mrs. Hart shouted from her porch across the street, over her chalk-drawing twins, "Au revoir!"

Barris got embarrassed, and apologized to Glenda, and recounted the story of why they moved to New Orleans six weeks prior.

"My mom found out she has French connections in her family history. All I hear now is 'Bonjour this' and 'Bonjour that.'"

"Ugh, tell me about it. We moved here from New Mexico because my mother's great-time-five grandfather was Spanish. But I don't really know any of the language, but a little. I was actually born here, we moved back to be closer to my father's family. But my mom still does everything in Spanish."

Barris laughed when she told the rest of her story, immediately feeling comfortable and at ease with her, when they compared their crazy mothers.

They walked down the fall leaf-covered road to school on that September morning and chatted it up before they met Dean and Pevy at the corner to all walk together.

The school bell rang off into the distance.

Finding a connection with someone is marvelous, the realization of knowing you have a friend is great, BUT to be understood by someone...is profound.

ABOUT THE
Author

B **randt Ricca** is a D.C.-based entrepreneur. Having a writing background and a family history of owning a newspaper, telling stories has always been at the forefront of Brandt's mindset.

Creating a narrative is a must for Brandt, who always wants to convey a message with events or imagery through his branding agency, Nora Lee by Brandt Ricca.

Brandt was born in Baton Rouge, Louisiana, and loves the Southern culture and creative atmosphere of New Orleans, which inspired the setting for the life of Barris Hart.

ABOUT THE

illustrator

Matt Miller is a designer and artist that bounces back and forth from D.C. and Florida. For as long as he can remember, Matt has had a passion for expressing his ideas and creativity in drawings and paintings. His artistic background and love for interior design and architecture are the foundation for his interior design and rendering business, Perspective.

With a soft spot for historic architecture of the American South, and gathering inspiration from his own vivid dreams, he felt he was the perfect fit for illustrating the world of the Barris Books series.

CPSIA information can be obtained
at www.ICGtesting.com
Printed in the USA
BVHW022009260921
617574BV00010B/58/J